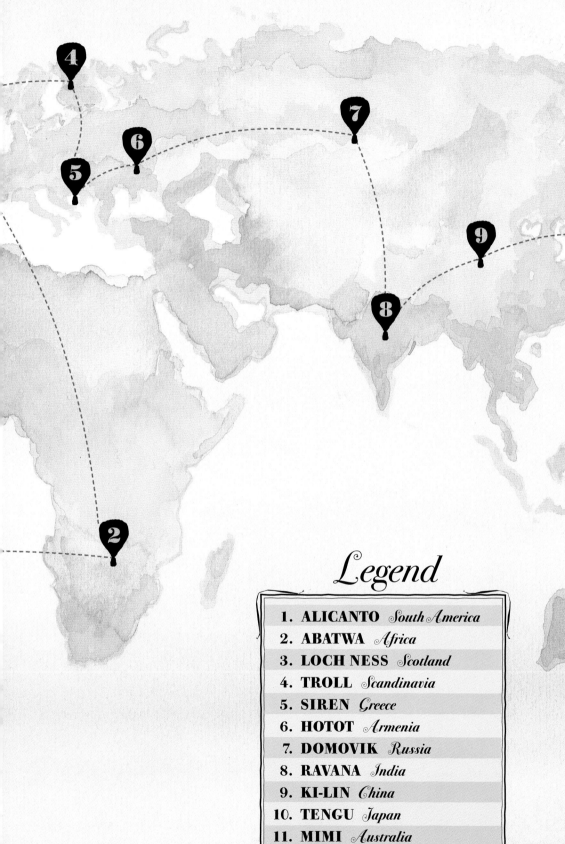

Legend

1. **ALICANTO** *South America*
2. **ABATWA** *Africa*
3. **LOCH NESS** *Scotland*
4. **TROLL** *Scandinavia*
5. **SIREN** *Greece*
6. **HOTOT** *Armenia*
7. **DOMOVIK** *Russia*
8. **RAVANA** *India*
9. **KI-LIN** *China*
10. **TENGU** *Japan*
11. **MIMI** *Australia*
12. **ADLET** *Greenland*
13. **SASQUATCH** *North America*

The Essential Worldwide MONSTER GUIDE

by **Linda Ashman**

illustrations by **David Small**

Simon & Schuster Books for Young Readers

SIMON & SCHUSTER BOOKS FOR YOUNG READERS

An imprint of Simon & Schuster Children's Publishing Division

1230 Avenue of the Americas, New York, New York 10020

SIMON & SCHUSTER BOOKS FOR YOUNG READERS is a trademark of Simon & Schuster.

Book design by Greg Stadnyk

The text of this book is set in Bodoni Old Face.

The illustrations are rendered in watercolor.

Manufactured in China

2 4 6 8 10 9 7 5 3 1

Library of Congress Cataloging-in-Publication Data

Ashman, Linda. The Essential Worldwide Monster Guide / by Linda Ashman ; illustrated by David Small.—1st ed. p. cm. ISBN 0-689-82640-0

1. Monsters—Juvenile poetry. 2. Children's poetry, American. [1. Monsters—Poetry. 2. American poetry. 3. Humorous poetry.] I. Title: Essential worldwide monster guide.

II. Small, David, 1945– , ill. III. Title. PS3551.S399 T73 2003 811'.6—dc21 00-046365

To Doree, Jeff, Lindsay, and Jenny with love
—L. A.

To Sarah
—D. S.

WELCOME TRAVELERS!

So . . . you're traveling far from home.
You've packed your toothbrush, camera, comb,
Your favorite hat, your lucky ring,
But have you thought of everything?

Are you prepared for hidden dangers:
Monsters, pranksters, spooky strangers?
Beasts with fangs and piercing claws,
Spiky horns and giant jaws?

Guaranteed—some day, some place—
You'll meet a monster face-to-face.
Don't destroy a great vacation—
Arm yourself with information!

With this handy monster guide,
You can take these beasts in stride.
Save yourself the stress and strife!
Save your spirit! Save your life!

Yes, for pleasant, pain-free trips,
Don't leave home without these tips!

ALICANTO ALERT

If you follow the bird,
The gold-eating bird,
He'll show you the way to the treasure.

If you follow the light
Of his wings through the night,
He'll lead you to wealth beyond measure.

If you follow him high
Up the cliff toward the sky,
To the peak where the riches glow,

You'll wave to the bird,
That mischievous bird,
As you plunge to the rocks below.

The **ALICANTO** is a South American bird who eats gold and silver deposits, and sometimes uses the golden light of his wings to lead fortune hunters astray, often over cliffs.

WATCH YOUR STEP!

The gentle Abatwa reside among ants.
They forage for food in the African plants.

Consider their safety when in their milieu:
You'll wipe out a village with one misplaced shoe.

THE **ABATWA** ARE DIMINUTIVE CREATURES, MUCH LIKE TINY HUMANS, WHO LIVE AMONG THE ANTHILLS OF SOUTHERN AFRICA.

$\mathscr{S}$HORE WARNING

Be careful near Loch Ness.
Don't wander off, oblivious.
Nessie likes the water,
But she just might be amphibious.

THE **LOCH NESS MONSTER,** ALSO KNOWN AS NESSIE, IS AN ENORMOUS
SERPENTLIKE CREATURE WHO LIVES IN THE WATERS OF LOCH NESS, SCOTLAND.

TROLL BRIDGE:
ALTERNATE ROUTE ADVISED

When you visit Grimley Palace,
You will come upon a moat.
There's a bridge that goes across it,
But it's best to take the boat.

Grimley Bridge is always guarded
By a nasty little troll.
If you choose to take the bridge,
The beast will ask you for a toll.

He might ask you for a quarter,
Or a cookie and some milk.
He might ask you for a whistle,
Or a jacket made of silk.

He might ask you for a cello,
Or a shiny pocketknife.
He might ask you for your mittens.
He might ask you for your life.

If you visit Grimley Palace,
You will have to cross the moat.
Skip the bridge that goes across it.
Don't be foolish! Take the boat!

TROLLS ARE NASTY, UNATTRACTIVE CREATURES FOUND IN SCANDINAVIA.
SOME LIVE UNDER BRIDGES AND REQUIRE PASSERSBY TO PAY COSTLY TOLLS.

FORGO THIS SHOW!

Behold the sleek Bird Ladies,
Here on the docks,
Singing their single,
"My Love's on the Rocks."

Critics say:
"Haunting!"
"Hypnotic!"
"A smash!"

The fans come in droves
(And depart with a *splash*!).

Cover your ears, or cling to the mast—
This one night of music
Could well be your last!

SIRENS ARE GREEK MONSTERS, PART BIRD AND PART WOMAN, WHO USE THEIR HAUNTINGLY BEAUTIFUL SONGS TO SHIPWRECK SAILORS.

How to spot a hotot

The hotot will lurk in the muckiest murk,
Devising unpleasant surprises.
Don't fall for his charm. Don't reach for his arm.
Get wise to the hotot's disguises.

The hotot is not very easy to spot,
You'll need a few clues to his ruse.
Observe his attire. It's speckled with mire.
His shoes ooze with swamp-puddle goos.

HOTOTS ARE EVIL SPIRITS FOUND IN ARMENIAN SWAMPS AND RIVERS. THEY TRY TO FOOL THEIR VICTIMS BY APPEARING AS PLEASANT, DANCING CREATURES, BUT ALWAYS HAVE SWAMP-MUCK ON THEIR CLOTHES.

BE A CONSIDERATE HOUSEGUEST

Don't bang about the kitchen.
Don't play annoying games.
Just leave a bit of supper . . .
Or the house goes up in flames.

THE **DOMOVIK** IS A RUSSIAN SPIRIT WHO GUARDS THE HOUSE, TYPICALLY FROM HIS PLACE BEHIND THE STOVE. HE IS EASILY OFFENDED, AND HAS BEEN KNOWN TO BURN THE HOUSE DOWN IF ANNOYED.

AVOID EXCESSIVE AFFECTION

Don't be duped by pleasant faces—
Dodge this demon's strong embraces.

Hugs are fine, in moderation.
Ten at once cause consternation.

RAVANA IS THE KING OF THE RAKSHASAS, A RACE OF DEMONS WHO LIVE IN INDIA. IN ONE OF HIS INCARNATIONS, RAVANA HAS TEN HEADS AND TWENTY ARMS.

PLEASE DON'T KISS THE KI-LIN!

Noble beast, a breed apart.
Known to warm the coldest heart.

If—enchanted by its grace—
You feel the urge to kiss its face,

Temper your exuberance!
Note the sharp protuberance!

Venture close and risk your fate—
That spiky horn can lacerate!

So I say, with some insistence:
Show your love . . . but from a distance.

THE **KI-LIN** IS A GENTLE, VIRTUOUS CREATURE FOUND IN CHINA. HE IS A COMPOSITE OF SEVERAL ANIMALS, INCLUDING A DEER, A LION, AND MOST NOTABLY, A UNICORN.

Quiet! Tengu Territory!

Tengu are bizarre, indeed—
A most peculiar hybrid breed.

Hatch like chicks from giant eggs,
But walk around on human legs.

Vicious-tempered, so I've heard,
Quite unlike the average bird.

Swoop from trees on soaring wings
(People rarely do such things).

Are they human, bird, or beast?
It doesn't matter in the least.

Let this motto be your guide:
When you see the tengu, HIDE!

TENGU ARE MISCHIEVOUS SPIRITS, PART BIRD AND PART HUMAN, FOUND IN THE MOUNTAINOUS REGIONS OF JAPAN.

Don't Feed the Mimi

They're light as a seed.
They're frail as a reed.
They knock themselves down with a sneeze.

They can't venture out
When storms are about
(They might blow away in the breeze!).

If they leave their cracks
And ask you for snacks,
Say NO! Do not let them indulge!

Although they're quite thin,
They won't squeeze back in
If their bellies should happen to bulge.

MIMIS ARE VERY LONG, THIN CREATURES WHO LIVE IN THE CRACKS OF ROCKY CLIFFS IN NORTHERN AUSTRALIA.

NEVER TRUST AN ADLET

Though you find the fellow friendly,
Like his smile (despite the drooling),
When he says, "I will not eat you,"
You can bet he's only fooling.

THE ADLET, A RACE OF MONSTROUS, MAN-EATING DOG
CREATURES, LIVE NEAR THE INUIT OF CANADA AND GREENLAND.

DON'T SNEER AT SASQUATCH

Sasquatch sings the Blizzard Blues:
Toes are frozen, has no shoes.
Icy teardrops sting his eyes.
Can't find clothes in Bigfoot size.

Be forewarned, you travel bug,
Wrapped in fleece, contented, snug.
Stop that smirking. Do not gloat.
In a flash, he'll snatch your coat.

SASQUATCH, ALSO KNOWN AS **BIGFOOT,** IS AN ENORMOUS,
FURRY CREATURE WHO LIVES IN THE SNOWY MOUNTAINS OF NORTH AMERICA.

SAFE AT LAST!

Tour is over! Homeward bound!
I see you've made it, safe and sound.
It's been a beastly trip, I'll bet!
Perhaps a few close calls, and yet
You've all survived the tour! How nice!
(Thanks, no doubt, to my advice!)

Now, heave a sigh; the danger's past.
We're on our way back home, at last.
Those monstrous beasts are gone from sight.
Sit back! Relax! Enjoy the flight!